P9-AOW-648

BOOK 2

Little Olympians

ATHENA, GODDESS OF WISDOM

This is a work of fiction. Any references to historical events, real people, or real places are used fictitiously. Other names, characters, places, and events are products of the author's imagination, and any resemblance to actual events or places or persons, living or dead, is entirely coincidental.

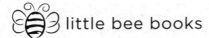 little bee books

New York, NY
Copyright © 2021 by Little Bee Books
All rights reserved, including the right of reproduction
in whole or in part in any form.
Manufactured in China RRD 0121
littlebeebooks.com

Library of Congress Cataloging-in-Publication Data is available upon request.
ISBN 978-1-4998-1151-3 (hc)
First Edition 10 9 8 7 6 5 4 3 2 1
ISBN 978-1-4998-1152-0 (pbk)
First Edition 10 9 8 7 6 5 4 3 2 1
ISBN 978-1-4998-1236-7 (ebook)

For information about special discounts on bulk purchases, please contact Little Bee Books at sales@littlebeebooks.com.

BOOK 2

Little OLYMPiANS

ATHENA, GODDESS OF WISDOM

BY A.I. NEWTON   ILLUSTRATED BY ANJAN SARKAR

Fountaindale Public Library District
300 W. Briarcliff Rd.
Bolingbrook, IL 60440

little bee books

TABLE OF CONTENTS

THE GODS OF OLYMPUS

Once, all-powerful gods ruled from their home atop the cloud-covered heights of Mount Olympus. Zeus, God of Thunder; Athena, Goddess of Wisdom; Apollo, the Sun God; Ares, God of Combat; Aphrodite, Goddess of Beauty and Nature; Poseidon, God of the Seas, and others possessed incredible powers, and controlled the fate of humans on Earth . . .

. . . but these powerful beings were not always the mighty gods of Olympus. Once, long ago, they were just a bunch of kids. . . .

CHAPTER 1
THE EUREKA OLYMPICS

Zeus, Athena, Aphrodite, Apollo, Artemis, Ares, and Hermes were young gods sent to Eureka by their parents to learn how to control their developing powers. One day, they all gathered around a long table in the dining room of the bunkhouse, their home away from home.

"That dinner was delicious!" said Zeus. Since arriving at Eureka for training several months earlier, Zeus's confidence in using his power of controlling thunder and lightning had grown.

"Yeah, but what's for dessert?" asked Hermes, the fastest of all the young gods at Eureka. "A meal is just not complete without dessert."

"It's a good thing you run as fast as you do," said Artemis, whose skill as an archer was improving every day. "With that sweet tooth of yours, you need a way to burn it all off."

"Well, we happen to have a very special dessert," said Athena. "Hestia, Goddess of Family and Hearth, baked us a fig and honey pie. You remember her. She was in the advanced group of gods that helped us battle the Cyclops."

"Ooh," said Hermes. "I've had her pies before. She is an excellent baker. Bring it on!"

Athena placed a still-steaming fig and honey pie in the center of the table. But before anyone could get a piece, the door to the bunkhouse flew open. In walked Centaur, a half man, half horse, who served as a mentor to the young gods at Eureka.

"Hello, Little Olympians! You're all needed outside immediately for an important announcement," he said.

"Race you!" shouted Ares, bolting from the table.

Everyone else followed, trying to push past one another to be the first one out the door.

On the large stone patio in front of the bunkhouse, Centaur and Poseidon were waiting. Poseidon was Zeus's older brother and also a counselor at Eureka.

"I see you all remain quite competitive with each other, even in something as simple as leaving a building," said Centaur once everyone had finally gathered. "But this is good, and Poseidon will tell you why."

Poseidon stepped forward to speak. "Tomorrow morning, we begin a series of highly competitive games which we like to call the Eureka Olympics—a long-standing tradition we have here," Poseidon began. "These contests are designed to help you learn how to think quickly as you face unexpected situations. You will need to use your powers thoughtfully and swiftly to succeed. Until tomorrow morning, then."

The young gods returned to the bunkhouse dining room excited about the games.

"Well, you know if any of the games call for great speed, I'll be the winner," Hermes boasted through a mouthful of pie.

"As long as it isn't a contest of strength," Apollo chimed in.

"That's right," said Ares. "Because I'm going to win *that* contest!"

"No way!" Apollo said.

"I've gotten much better at aiming my lightning bolts," said Zeus. "So I hope one of the challenges involves hitting a target."

"If it does, I'll be right there with you," said Artemis, pulling an arrow from the quiver on her back, loading up her bow, and firing. The arrow streaked across the room, went right through the handle of a metal cup resting on a nearby table, and pinned the cup to the far wall.

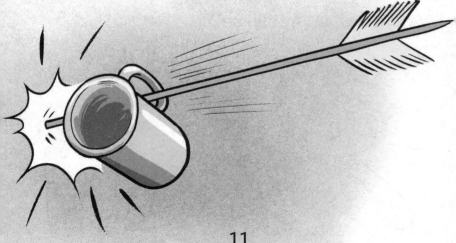

"Well, if nature is involved in one of the games, that game will be mine!" said Aphrodite. She pointed a finger at a vining plant. The plant grew two feet taller in a matter of seconds.

Zeus noticed Athena sitting alone quietly as the others all boasted about their abilities.

"What about you, Athena?" Zeus asked. "What kind of game will you win?"

Before Athena could reply, Apollo jumped in: "I guess if there's a petteia match, she's got it made, being the Goddess of Wisdom and all." Apollo made air quotes with his fingers when he said the word "wisdom."

"My parents like to play petteia," said Zeus. "It's a really hard board game with lots of strategy involved. I couldn't even figure out how to make the first move."

Athena smiled, then got up and walked outside without saying a word.

"I hope she's okay," said Zeus, watching his friend leave.

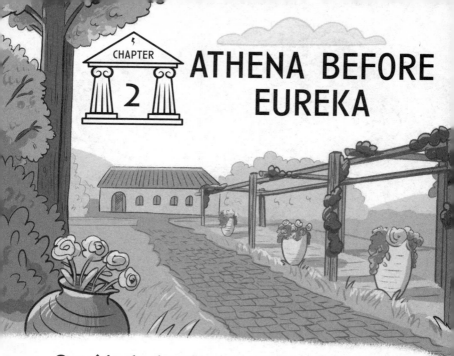

CHAPTER 2

ATHENA BEFORE EUREKA

Outside the bunkhouse, Athena wandered through a garden as the sun began to set. *All this talk of who has what power is bringing up stuff I haven't thought about in a while,* she thought to herself.

Her mind flashed back to when she was younger, growing up in a seaside cottage along Mount Olympus's shoreline.

She thought about the conversation that led to her coming to Eureka. Athena had been strolling along the beach with her mother, Metis, a sea nymph. Metis had scaly skin and flippers instead of feet. She was equally at home on land or in the water.

"I am concerned, Athena," Metis had said. "You have reached the age when other young gods begin to discover their powers, and yet no evidence of power has emerged in you."

"But how can I know if my power is getting stronger if I don't even know what it's supposed to be?" Athena asked. "Don't all things happen in their own time? Doesn't trouble come from trying to force something you think *should* be rather than allowing what *is* to develop?"

Metis smiled. "You are wise beyond your years, young one," she said. "Perhaps that is why, even at your young age, I already cannot beat you at petteia! And I know that when you set your mind to something, nothing can break your sharp focus."

"So we wait, right?" Athena asked. "And in time, my power will reveal itself?"

"Maybe," said Metis, "but I have another idea. Many of your friends have already left Mount Olympus to go to Eureka to learn to control their powers."

Athena sighed. "But those young gods already knew what their powers were before they went to Eureka. What good would going to Eureka do if I don't even know what my power is?"

"Well, I'm hoping that maybe the teachers there can help you figure that out," Metis replied.

Athena grew very quiet and thought this through. She watched the waves crash onto the shore and weighed her mother's words carefully.

"Going to Eureka sounds like a wise course of action," Athena finally said. "I agree."

Standing now in the garden at Eureka and staring at a blooming purple iris, Athena smiled at how right she had been. Her time at Eureka did indeed help her discover that the great wisdom, focus, and creativity she had been born with *were* her powers.

Comforted by this memory, Athena strode confidently back into the bunkhouse.

Seeing her, Zeus asked, "Are you okay?"

"We thought maybe you were trying to get a head start on the petteia competition," Apollo quipped.

"You know, Apollo . . . despite what everyone says, you *are* a smart guy," Athena replied.

"Thanks," Apollo said, smiling at first, then scrunching up his face and looking slightly confused. "I think."

"It is wise of you to realize that *every* competition is essentially a petteia match," Athena explained. "A game of thought and strategy. Regardless of what the actual contest may be, understanding the best way to approach whatever challenge one faces is the key to victory."

"Uh-huh," Apollo said, nodding, but not really understanding what Athena had just said. "But I can still beat you if the contest is to see who can lift the heaviest object."

"We'll see," Athena said confidently. "We'll see."

24

CHAPTER 3
LET THE GAMES BEGIN!

The next morning, the Eureka Olympics began. Out on the patio, Poseidon addressed the young gods.

"Welcome to the Eureka Olympics! Remember, these are only games; however, they have been designed to encourage you to use your powers in a creative manner. We will all meet at the entrance to the forest path in one hour. There, the first competition will be a footrace."

Hermes smiled. "I got that won already," he said.

"And I'll be with you every step of the way," said Apollo.

"Me, too. Just because we haven't beaten you in a footrace yet doesn't mean we won't today," added Ares.

A plan quickly formed in Athena's mind.

Zeus frowned. "Well, I don't stand a chance against those guys, Athena," he said. But when he looked over at her, Athena was gone.

"Maybe she's hiding until the race is over, since she knows I'm going to win," Hermes said, smiling.

"Don't be so sure of that," said Artemis. "Athena's got great wisdom."

"Yeah," said Ares, "but she has to run with her *feet*, not her *brain*."

Athena hurried to the large kitchen area near the back of the bunkhouse. There, she found Hestia. As usual, Hestia was busy baking.

"Hello, Athena," said Hestia, pulling a steaming loaf of freshly baked bread from a stone hearth. "Nice to see you again."

"You as well, Hestia," said Athena. "I have come to ask for your help."

"Of course," said Hestia.

"I'm wondering if you have any more of those delicious fig and honey pies?" Athena asked.

"I made a few this very morning," replied Hestia.

"May I take some?" Athena asked.

"Help yourself," said Hestia as she slipped an unbaked loaf of bread into the hearth.

"Thank you," said Athena, gathering up a few pies in her arms. Then she hurried off.

Hermes has a sweet tooth that he just can't control, Athena thought. *I can use that to my advantage.*

She took some long, thin pieces of wood and quickly painted a few signs. Then she slipped the pies and the signs into a sack and hurried to the forest's main path.

Whenever she came to a side path, she pulled out one of the wooden signs and attached it to a tree. She hung several more of these signs on branches leading to even smaller paths and placed a pie at the end of each one. Then she snuck back out of the forest and arrived at the entrance to the main path in time for the start of the race.

CHAPTER 4
ON YOUR MARK, GET SET . . .

The young gods lined up at the start of the main forest path.

"Hey, where did you go?" Zeus asked Athena.

"I was just uh, preparing for the race," she said.

Poseidon spoke up. "On your mark . . . get set . . . GO!"

The young gods all took off sprinting. Not surprisingly, Hermes, Apollo, and Ares quickly sped ahead of the pack.

A few minutes later, Hermes had left even Apollo and Ares behind and was out in front by himself. "I got this one in the bag," he said aloud, increasing his lead.

That's when he spotted the first sign hanging from a low tree limb.

FIG AND HONEY
PIE THIS WAY!

"No way!" Hermes shouted to himself, slowing to a stop. "I do love fig and honey pie! And heck, I'm fast enough that I have time to eat some pie and still win the race."

He grabbed the sign and tossed it into some bushes. "And, I want the pie all for myself!" He hurried down the small side path.

That's when Apollo and Ares spotted him.

"Look, it's Hermes!" cried Apollo.

"I bet he knows a shortcut that will help him win the race," said Ares.

"Come on," Apollo shouted. "Let's follow him and use the shortcut ourselves!"

Not too long after, Athena raced past the spot where the three leaders had gotten off the main path. With them gone now, Athena surged into the lead and crossed the finish line first.

A few minutes later, Hermes—his hands and face all sticky from pie—came running across the finish line, followed closely by Apollo and Ares.

"How in Eureka did you beat me, Athena?" Hermes asked.

"All I can say is . . . victory is sweet," replied Athena. "And speaking of sweet, how did you like the pie?"

"The pie was great, but—" Hermes paused as a wide smile began to spread across Athena's face.

"Nice trick," Hermes groaned. "And nice pie, too! Hestia again, right?"

Athena nodded.

"Pretty clever," said Hermes, licking his fingers.

"I told you that wisdom can be a valuable power," Athena said.

Apollo and Ares did not appreciate Athena's cleverness as much as Hermes did.

"Not only was that side path not a shortcut, it added time to our run," cried Apollo.

"Yeah, and we didn't even get any pie!" moaned Ares.

Hermes smiled and rubbed his belly.

CHAPTER 5 READY, AIM, FIRE!

At lunch, Apollo was still annoyed.

"You kind of cheated, you know," Apollo said to Athena.

"Not at all," chimed in Artemis, his twin sister. "Athena simply used her power to win the contest. Her cleverness and wisdom proved more effective than your speed."

"And that pie *was* good," said Hermes. "In fact, I almost didn't have enough room for lunch." He grabbed a piece of bread and a hunk of cheese and shoved them both into his mouth. "Almost," he said through a mouthful of food.

After lunch, the young gods gathered in an apple orchard. Poseidon explained the second competition.

"In order to continue to participate in the Eureka Olympics, each of you must knock an apple off of that tree," he said, pointing to a tree filled with apples two hundred yards away.

"And not just any apple," Poseidon continued. "You have each been assigned a specific apple to hit. Anyone who does not remove their apple from the tree will be eliminated from the games."

"I'll go first," said Artemis, whose skill as an archer was already reaching legendary levels. "This will only take a moment."

She grabbed an arrow from her quiver and loaded her bow. Then she raised it, aimed, and fired. Her arrow sailed straight and true. It pierced her apple dead center, knocking it cleanly off the tree.

Watching the great skill of Artemis, Athena realized that there was no way she could shoot her apple off the tree with a bow and arrow from this far away. Once again, she would have to use *her* power if she was going to succeed.

She leaned in close to Apollo. "Well, it's obvious that your sister is a way better archer than you are," she whispered in his ear.

"Oh, yeah?" said Apollo. "Well, we'll see when my turn comes."

"I'll go next," said Ares.

He picked up a rock and unleashed a powerful throw. The rock sped through the air and slammed into his apple, knocking it from the tree.

"Not everyone needs to shoot an arrow," Ares said.

That gave Hermes an idea.

"I'll throw a rock, too," Hermes said.

Ares laughed. "Since when do you have the strength to throw something that far?"

"Watch me!" said Hermes.

Hermes picked up a rock and hurled it. Then he ran toward the tree at blinding speed, hoping he could get to the tree and back before anyone noticed he was gone.

Outrunning his rock, he reached the tree and knocked his apple off with his hand. Then he sped back to the other young gods.

"Athena is not the only smart one around here," Hermes whispered to himself. "I may have just tricked my way into staying in the competition."

CHAPTER 6

TARGET TIME

Poseidon frowned, not fooled at all by what Hermes had done. He thought for a moment and spoke.

"Although your rock did not hit the apple, you did use your power of great speed to complete the task. Your cleverness is appreciated. You may continue in the games, Hermes."

Athena again whispered to Apollo. "You see? Sometimes, cleverness wins," she said. "But I still think you don't have the skill your sister has."

Apollo started fuming. "Just wait until my turn!"

Aphrodite was up next. She closed her eyes and concentrated deeply. As the Goddess of Nature, she had the power to communicate with every living being, including plants. She now focused her mind on the apple tree and spoke directly to it.

"My friend, I need you to shake your third branch up, but only that branch. Now!"

The branch containing Aphrodite's apple began to shake up and down, then side to side. Her apple dropped to the ground.

"Nice," said Zeus.

"You are next," Aphrodite replied.

Zeus extended his hands and focused on the branch holding his apple. He took a deep breath. As he exhaled, he released a bolt of lightning that sliced the entire branch off the tree. It crashed to the ground with a loud thud.

"Well, you did get your apple," said Hermes with a laugh. "And about twenty others!"

"I think you should go next," Athena said to Apollo, ready to put her plan into action. "Though I doubt you can even reach the tree with one of your arrows. You're certainly not the archer that your sister is."

"I can hit as many apples on as many trees as you pick," Apollo shouted, getting flustered and red-faced.

"Well, there is no way in Eureka or Olympus that you could possibly knock down both your apple and my apple with one shot."

"Oh, yeah!" yelled Apollo. "You just watch me!"

Seething, Apollo snatched an arrow from his quiver and fired. The arrow streaked directly to the tree, where it knocked off both his apple and Athena's.

"There!" he shouted, glaring at Athena. "I did it!"

"Well, foolish me," Athena said. "I was wrong. I guess I'm not as smart as everyone thinks I am."

"I guess you're not!" said Apollo with a smirk.

That's when everyone started laughing as they all caught on to how Athena had just tricked Apollo into helping her remain in the Eureka Olympics.

As Apollo slowly realized what had just happened, even he started laughing, too.

CHAPTER 7
THE BOULDER ROLL

"I have to say that you really got me today, Athena," Apollo admitted that evening at dinner. "But let me ask you one question: Could you have shot that apple off the tree by yourself?"

"I doubt it," Athena admitted. "Archery is not my best skill."

"So you really shouldn't be allowed to continue onto the next contest," Apollo said, "since *you* didn't actually knock your apple down."

"I think what Athena did was brilliant," said Zeus. "She used her power to knock her apple off the tree. That was the challenge. Poseidon didn't say that she had to shoot the apple with an arrow."

"Or shoot a lightning bolt," added Aphrodite.

"Or throw a rock," said Hermes.

"Or talk to the tree," said Artemis.

Apollo frowned. "I guess," he said.

The next morning, the young gods gathered at the base of a steep mountain where a series of large boulders were lined up.

"The next challenge is quite simple in concept, although difficult in execution," Poseidon explained. "Each of you will attempt to get one of these boulders to the top of this mountain. I do not expect you all to succeed, but I do expect you all to try."

Zeus chose a boulder and pressed his shoulder against it. Straining, he grit his teeth and started to push the heavy rock up the steep slope.

When he was about a third of the way up the mountain, Zeus ran out of strength. He stumbled and his boulder rolled back down the mountain.

"Well, I tried," he said.

Hermes went next. He took a running start, grabbing a boulder while moving at full speed. His extra momentum helped him move the heavy rock about halfway up the slope. But the angle of the mountain and the weight of the boulder proved too much for him. As he started to slide back down, he let the boulder go.

"Man, that is tough!" he cried.

Artemis then took her turn. She managed to roll her boulder up the slope a short way, but her hands grew weak and her shoulders ached. She, too, was forced to release it and let the boulder roll back down.

"Is anyone going to be able to do this?" Artemis asked aloud.

Ares and Apollo each wrapped their arms around a boulder and steadily inched their way up the mountain.

"We're the only ones strong enough to do this," Ares boasted.

"I think the others just proved that," added Apollo.

"Haven't you learned yet that winning every contest isn't always just about strength?" asked Aphrodite.

In a flash, she sped right past Ares and Apollo, easily rolling her boulder.

"How are you *doing* that?" Apollo cried, straining under the weight of his boulder.

"She's using her power," said Ares. "Look!"

With her connection to nature, Aphrodite created a path of wet, green moss under her boulder. Using the slippery surface, she pushed her boulder up the steep slope with ease. In a few minutes, she became the first to reach the top.

"Humph," grumbled Apollo, struggling, but refusing to give up. "Where's Athena? What's she up to?"

"Right here," Athena replied, hurrying up the mountain past Apollo. She was not pushing a boulder. Instead, she held a metal wheel and a long length of rope.

"Didn't you forget something?" asked Ares. "Like, oh, I don't know . . . a boulder, maybe?"

"No, I have everything I need right here," Athena replied as she sped up the mountain.

Near the top, Apollo finally ran out of strength. He released his boulder, and it tumbled back down to the base of the mountain. He followed it down, dejected.

Ares kept going. He was just about at the top when he saw Athena hurrying back down, now holding both ends of her long rope.

"See you at the bottom," Athena said.

"Not until I get this boulder all the way up," Ares groaned, continuing his slow and steady trek.

Arriving at the bottom of the mountain, Athena tied one end of her rope to her boulder and the other end to a second boulder. The center of the rope reached up to the top of the mountain, where Athena had attached a metal pulley using the wheel.

She rolled one of the boulders to the edge of a nearby cliff and pushed it over. As the boulder fell, it lifted the other boulder it was tied to up the side of the mountain using the pulley. Her boulder arrived at the top a few seconds before Ares finished his climb.

"You tricked us again!" Apollo shouted, standing at the bottom next to Athena. "At least Ares got his boulder all the way to the top the right way—using his strength!"

"All we had to do was get our boulder to the top any way we chose," Athena replied. "I did it. Aphrodite did it. And Ares did it."

"Athena is correct," Poseidon said, addressing the whole group. "Well done, once again."

CHAPTER 8 — LET IT GROW!

At breakfast the next morning, the young gods noticed that Apollo was missing.

"Do you know where he is?" Zeus asked Ares, Apollo's best friend.

"No, I'm as surprised as—" Ares stopped midsentence as he spotted Apollo outside, running past the huge dining room window. "There he is."

"Looks like he's getting in some extra exercise before this morning's challenge," Ares said.

"Too bad he can't do push-ups for his brain," said Hermes. "Because that's how Athena keeps beating him."

"Just using my true power like the rest of you," Athena said.

"Yeah, but your 'true power' doesn't really *do* anything," replied Ares.

"That is not true," Athena said. "The mentors here at Eureka helped me realize that."

"Besides," Aphrodite said, putting her arm around Athena's shoulders. "I don't know what you were watching these past few days, but I saw Athena do everything that was asked of her—and succeed every time!"

Before Ares could reply, Apollo burst into the room, sweating and out of breath.

"I'm ready for today's competition!" he said, huffing and puffing.

After breakfast, the young gods joined Poseidon outside on the patio.

"Today's competition is of a different nature than the previous ones," Poseidon announced. "Today, each of you will create your own garden."

"Good thing you did all that extra running this morning," Hermes whispered to Apollo, who sneered back at him.

"You may use plants you find around Eureka or any materials you like," explained Poseidon. "Begin!"

The young gods ran off in different directions, gathering the materials they would need to create their gardens.

Apollo grabbed a hoe and began tilling an open patch of ground.

"My butterfly garden will be a sure winner," he said confidently.

When he had churned up enough soil, Apollo took a shovel and started digging up flowering plants that he had seen butterflies perch on. He moved those plants into his garden and soon had butterflies landing on colorful flowers.

At the same time, Ares hauled buckets of sand from the shoreline, dumped them into one big pile, and started spreading the sand out in a curving pattern. Then he placed rocks throughout the sand and traced lines leading from one rock to the next.

"I bet no one else will think of creating a meditation garden!" he said when he had finished.

Hermes cleared a patch of ground, removing all the weeds and rocks. Then he planted all kinds of vegetables.

"Just planting these veggies makes me hungry!" he said.

Zeus dug a small pond and filled it with water. Then he hurried to a nearby lake where he gathered water lilies and carefully brought them back and placed the delicate floating plants into his pond.

"Poseidon's got to like this garden!"
Zeus said. "It's all about water."

Artemis filled her garden with fruit
trees. "Not only will I be able to eat the
fruit," she said, "but they'll make good
target practice, too!"

Aphrodite looked at all the gardens.

"You have all done well," she said.

Then she focused her mind and used her power to bring a magnificent garden into bloom. She watched as fruit appeared on trees, vegetables popped out of the ground, flowers opened, water flowed, and rocks arranged themselves in a pattern calming to the eye. She had created a lush, beautiful garden based on everyone else's ideas combined.

Athena watched closely as Aphrodite worked her magic.

I don't know how anyone can beat Aphrodite, thought Athena. *I'm not going to be able to think my way out of this one . . . unless . . .*

Athena smiled to herself and got busy putting together the worst garden ever. She dug up the ground, leaving clumps of dirt and grass everywhere. She stuck dead trees, shriveled flowers, and rotten vegetables into the messy earth. When she finished, she stepped back and admired her horrible garden.

"Looks like Athena's smarts couldn't help her this time," Apollo whispered to Ares. "That's the ugliest garden I've ever seen."

Aphrodite walked over to inspect her friend's garden. A look of horror crossed her face the moment she saw the mess that Athena had created.

"What in the name of Olympus happened here?" Aphrodite cried.

"I'm no good at this," Athena said, pretending to be upset. "I guess I'll have to settle for coming in last in this competition."

"Well, *I* won't settle," said Aphrodite. "I can't stand even *looking* at this mess. Even now, I can hear the plants calling out for my help."

Aphrodite closed her eyes and breathed deeply. The dead trees sprouted healthy green leaves, the shriveled flowers opened and burst into rainbows of color, and vegetables ripened in seconds into a hearty bounty.

"Thanks," Athena said to Aphrodite, smiling and winking.

"Sure, well I . . ." Aphrodite stopped. Then she started laughing. "You got me to do that, didn't you?"

Athena stayed silent. She raised her eyebrows and smiled back at her friend.

Poseidon arrived.

"You have all done very well," he said. "I call this contest a tie—Aphrodite and Athena are the winners. With an honorable mention to Zeus for playing to the judge."

Zeus blushed slightly but was glad his brother noticed what he had done.

AN A-MAZE-ING CONTEST

The final day of the Eureka Olympics arrived. The young gods all gathered in a large field. Filling the field was a maze made up of ten-foot-high, tightly trimmed shrub walls.

Poseidon addressed the young gods at the entrance to the maze.

"The goal of this final event is simple," he began. "You must enter the hedge maze here at the entrance and get to the exit on the other end of the maze. Begin!"

The young gods all hurried into the maze. Once inside, all anyone could see were tall, leafy green walls covered in colorful vining flowers.

The maze path branched off in many directions. The gods all scattered, starting their own individual journeys to find the exit.

Aphrodite strolled calmly through the maze. At each point where she had to choose a direction, she used her powers to reach out to the flowers growing on the maze walls.

"Left, right, or straight, my dears?" she asked.

All the flowers facing her slowly bent to the left.

"Thank you," said Aphrodite, taking the path on her left and continuing through the maze. Using her power, she became the first to emerge from the exit.

Meanwhile, Apollo raced frantically through the maze. After a few minutes, he realized that he was completely lost.

"How am I going to get through this thing?" he grumbled to himself. "It's impossible, no matter how fast or strong I am."

At that very moment, Apollo spotted an arrow soaring through the air above him.

"Artemis!" cried Apollo. "She's trying to show me the way!"

Apollo continued, moving in the direction from which the arrow had come.

Returning the favor for his sister, Apollo fired an arrow of his own straight up into the air to help guide her. The two continued to signal each other until they met at the maze's exit.

"Well, that wasn't so hard," Apollo said, stepping out of the maze.

"Not with a little help, it wasn't," added Artemis.

   Back in the maze, Zeus kept moving, turning left and right, without any real idea of where he was going or where he had already been.

   Then he got an idea.

   He raised his arms into the air, then pulled them down slowly. A dark rain cloud formed directly over his head. Rain poured down behind him as he moved forward, marking the path to show where he had already been.

   "Now, at least I won't retrace my steps anymore," Zeus said.

Not surprisingly, Hermes believed that his great speed would allow him to explore all the twists and turns of the maze until he found the way out. But after a few minutes, he realized that he was no closer to the end than when he had started.

Ahead, something rustled in the hedges.

"It must be a Minotaur, guardian monster of the maze!" Hermes cried. "I'm lost, and the Minotaur is going to get me!"

Frozen with fear, Hermes watched as a bunny hopped from the hedge and nibbled on some grass. Embarrassed and glad that none of his friends were there to see him, he continued forward.

When Zeus finally emerged from the maze's exit, he saw Aphrodite, Apollo, and Artemis.

"Where's Athena?" Zeus asked.

"Right here," Athena called out.

The other young gods turned and saw Athena sitting under an apple tree munching on an apple. Poseidon stood beside her, smiling. Athena waved.

"Athena has won the contest," said Poseidon. "And once again, she has used unconventional thinking."

"What does that mean?" asked Apollo, annoyed that Athena had seemingly outsmarted him again.

"I simply walked through the hedge wall and strolled along the outside of the maze to the exit," Athena explained. "No one said that we *had* to use the maze path."

Poseidon nodded. "All I said was that you had to get from the entrance to the exit. I said nothing about having to navigate your way through the maze."

Apollo just shook his head.

"But where's Ares?" asked Zeus.

As if in answer to Zeus's question, Ares came bursting through the wall of the maze. He was covered in scratches from muscling his way through the hedge.

"Who won?" Ares asked, pulling leaves out of his hair.

"Athena," replied Zeus. "She just walked through the hedge and around to the exit."

"What!?" Ares cried. "That's what I ended up doing. I could have just done that at the start!"

"But *you* didn't think of it," says Athena. "I did!"

Suddenly, a cry came from inside the maze.

"Help! I'm lost in here!"

"Hermes!" Zeus shouted.

"Will somebody please get me out of this maze!"

THE POWER OF WISDOM

That evening, a celebratory feast was held in the bunkhouse marking the end of the Eureka Olympics. Poseidon and Centaur joined the young gods.

"So, I'm a little confused," Apollo said. "Who won the Eureka Olympics?"

"Actually, you all did," said Poseidon. "The games were never meant to discover who the 'best' god was. There is no such thing. All each of you can hope to be is the best god *you* can be, using the gifts *you* have. One set of gifts is no better than another."

"Poseidon is correct," said Centaur. "The point of the games was for all of you to realize that you each have different strengths. Developing those strengths so that they serve you in the future is the very reason you are here at Eureka."

"It took me many years to realize exactly what my power was," Athena explained. "Growing up, my mom worried that my true power had not yet emerged. Yet I could beat her at petteia ever since the second time I played it. And I came up with solutions to problems that the adults in my life were struggling with. It took me a long time to realize that wisdom, the ability to form strategies and the understanding of other people, was indeed my gift."

"You sure proved that today," moaned Ares, still smarting from his scratches and cuts.

"I guess you weren't using tricks after all," admitted Apollo. "Even though I'd still like to actually beat you at something!"

"Athena took her knowledge and smarts and used them in each contest so that the rest of our powers didn't really matter and couldn't be used to beat her," said Zeus.

"So knowledge really is power," said Hermes, filling his mouth with fresh vegetables from Athena's garden.

Once again, Athena thought back to the days when she worried when her true power would emerge. She smiled now, thinking about how far she had come since then.

"And I can't think of a better group of friends to share my power with!" she said. "Now, Hermes, why don't you share some of those vegetables with the rest of us before you eat them all yourself!"

Look for more books by these creators...

...and read on for a sneak peek at the third book in the Little Olympians series

HERMES, THE FASTEST GOD

AN EXCITING JOURNEY

Hermes could not have been more excited. He and his fellow young gods were about to go on their first field trip since arriving at Eureka. He climbed into a golden carriage alongside Zeus, Athena, Apollo, Ares, Aphrodite, and Artemis. Beside them sat Poseidon. He was their counselor and also Zeus's big brother.

He tightly held reins that were attached to a team of six flying horses, led by Pegasus. At a command from Poseidon, the horses leapt from the ground, spread their mighty wings, and lifted the golden carriage high into the sky above Eureka.

"Welcome to your first field trip," Poseidon said. "We are going to the city of Argos in Greece. There, you will get your first glimpse at the humans whose fate you will control once you have grown up, fully realized your powers, and taken your place alongside the other gods of Mount Olympus.

"This trip will help you see that your powers exist for a reason," Poseidon explained as they soared through the clouds. "They are only important if they can be used to help the mortals who live around us. And so, the time has come for you to observe them up close."

"Cool!" said Zeus, lightning crackling

from his fingertips. "Wait until these humans get a load of my lightning and thunder."

"Never mind that," said Hermes. "Wait until they see how fast I can run!"

"They won't care about that once they see how strong I am!" boasted Ares.

Poseidon remained quiet, but Athena looked very concerned.

"Um, I don't think that's what Poseidon has in mind," she said.

Hermes saw Poseidon frown. "Well, at least *one* of you has some sense!" Poseidon boomed. "You cannot let the humans find out who you really are. The time for you to make an impact on their lives will come, but to reveal yourself now would mean banishment from Eureka and exile from *ever* ruling on Mount Olympus. Have I made myself clear?"

Artemis, the great archer, looked at Athena and nodded. She put her bow down beside her.

It's going to be really hard for me to not show off my power! Hermes thought.

"Don't worry, brother, we won't let you down," said Zeus.

"Good," said Poseidon. "Because we have arrived."

The carriage descended through the clouds. Soon, the Greek countryside came into view.

"Wow!" said Aphrodite, Goddess of Beauty and Nature. "I bet they grow some beautiful flowers down there. I can't wait to see them!"

This drew a stern look from Poseidon.

"Without drawing any attention to myself, of course," Aphrodite added quickly, as the carriage approached the ground.